To my grandmother Roza   D.K.
In memory of Rene and Harry   K.E.

Text by Elena Pasquali
Illustrations copyright © 2007 Dubravka Kolanovic
This edition copyright © 2007 Lion Hudson

The moral rights of the author and illustrator
have been asserted

A Lion Children's Book
an imprint of
Lion Hudson plc
Mayfield House, 256 Banbury Road,
Oxford OX2 7DH, England
www.lionhudson.com
ISBN 978 0 7459 6047 0

First edition 2007
1 3 5 7 9 10 8 6 4 2 0

A catalogue record for this book is available
from the British Library

Typeset in 22/38 Old Claude
Printed and bound in China

Safely through the Night

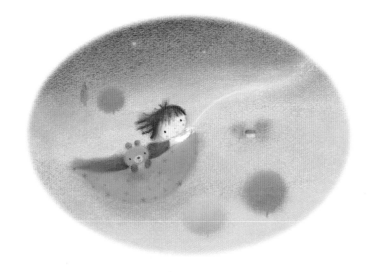

Safely through the Night

Elena Pasquali

Illustrated by
Dubravka Kolanovic

LION
CHILDREN'S

Emily sat up in bed for one
last look at the night sky.

'See,' she said to Cinnamon
Bear. 'A shooting star.'

A star tumbled through the
dark.

Then it was time to snuggle down with Hug, the quilt.

'Sweet dreams, Cinnamon Bear,' said Emily.

'And Hug: stay on the bed please.'

Together they fell asleep.

In the night, a starbeam came
and tapped at the window.

The noise woke them up, so
Emily went to let the starbeam
inside.

As she pulled it in, it looped
down into her hand, so she began
to wind it up like wool.

It looped and drooped so much
that Emily just had to keep on
winding.

Then came a gust of wind, and all at once Emily found herself floating through the air winding her ball of starbeam.

'We're here with you,' cried Cinnamon Bear.

Hug wrapped snugly around them, and on they flew.

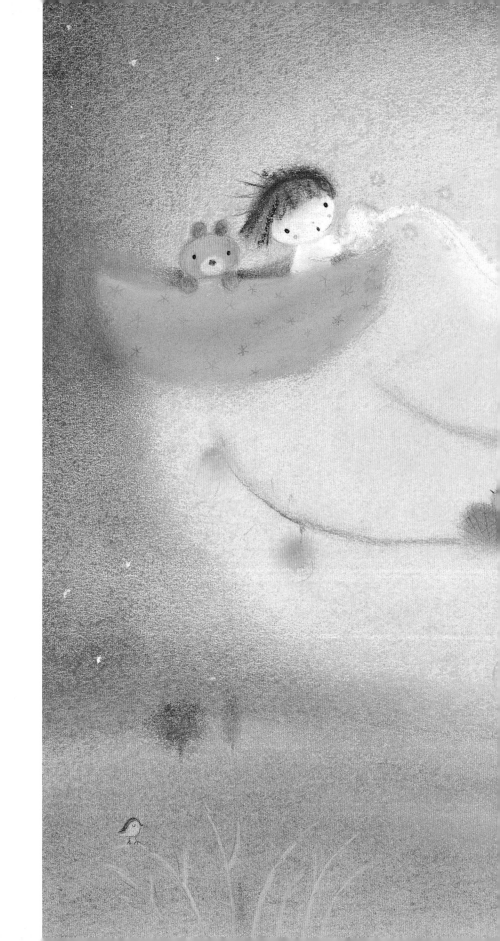

The starbeam dipped and dangled, and then it looped round an apple tree, turning the leaves to gold.

'You're up late,' chirruped a sleepy sparrow.

'I know, but there's this muddle to sort,' replied Emily.

'Take care!' said the sparrow as she watched them all fly by.

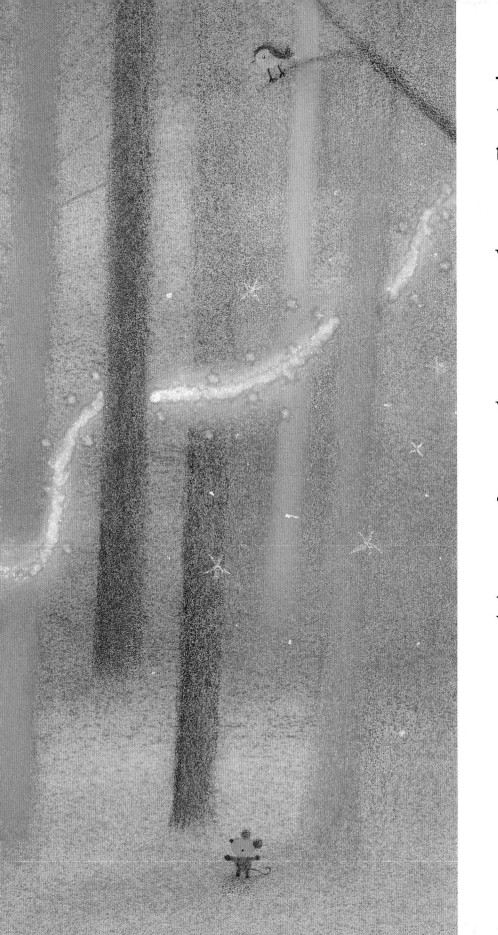

Now the starbeam trailed down to a deep dark wood.

From its tree, an owl looked on with big amber eyes.

'Hoo! hoo! hoo!' it laughed.

Some mice looked up from the woodland floor and giggled.

'Hee! hee! hee!' they squeaked. 'What fun!'

'Is this fun?' Cinnamon asked Emily. He looked a bit scared.

'Be brave,' said Emily. 'If you try to untie the tangles, I will be able to wind faster.'

As they flew through the night-time sky, Emily and Cinnamon kept winding, faster and faster.

They wound so fast that the starbeam pulled tight and then...

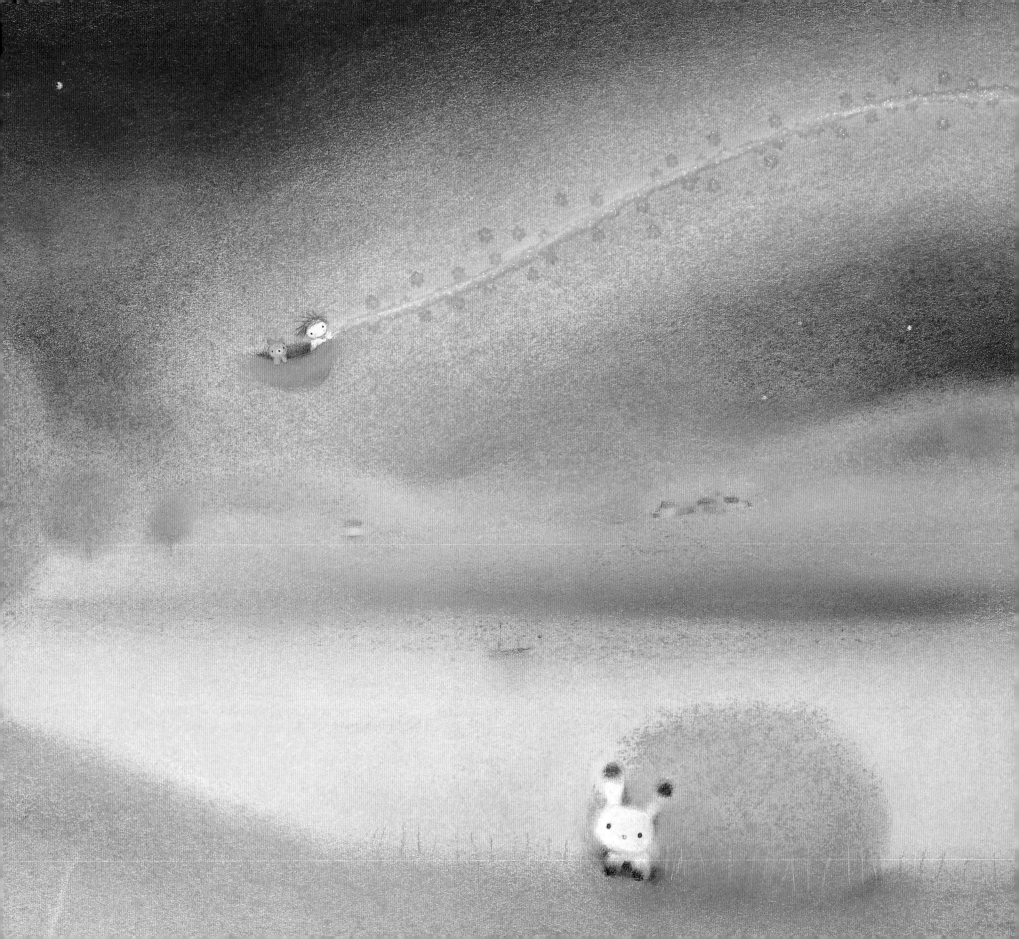

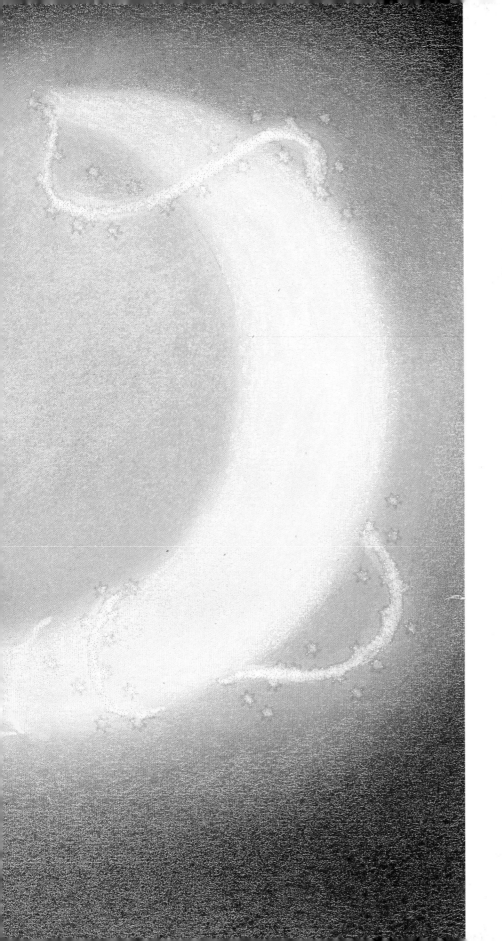

'Twing!'

The string pulled Emily, Cinnamon and Hug high into the sky.

'Oh look!' said Emily, 'The starbeam has got tangled on the moon.'

Then she heard a voice. 'It's all because of me.'

Emily looked around. It was an angel, about as big as her.

'I dropped a starball,' said the angel sorrowfully. 'Granny had just finished knitting with one, and I went to fetch her another.'

'We've wound it back up for you,' said Emily. 'Here you are.'

The little angel smiled and took Emily and Cinnamon and Hug to meet her granny.

'Thank you so much!' said the Granny angel. 'You have been kind. It must have taken you all night to wind so much.'

She reached down into her workbag and felt for something. 'Here,' she said. 'This is for you.'

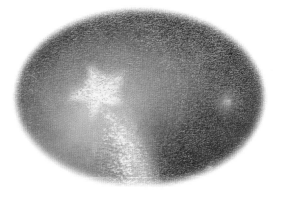

It was a knitted ball… dark and soft, yet somehow glowing.

'It's just so pretty,' said Emily. 'Oh look… now it's turning bright gold!'

All at once Emily was awake in bed with Cinnamon by her side and Hug all around her... and the golden sun was waking in a pink and blue morning sky.

Other titles from Lion Children's Books

Angel Shoes

Emily Pound and Sanja Rescek

My Very First Bedtime Book

Lois Rock and Alex Ayliffe

Ituku's Christmas Journey

Elena Pasquali and Dubravka Kolanovic